✱*MA(

Copyright © 2022 Judith S
ISBN: 9798356486791
All Rights Reserved
Printed in the USA
Cover design by Christy Aldridge
Edited by Makency Hudson

The events, characters, and locations in this book are all fictional. Any resemblance to reality is unintended and coincidental.

WARNING: *Magick* is an extreme, dark, and grotesque story. There are many graphic sequences of torture, gore, abuse, rape, and horror throughout.

⁂MAGICK⁂

MAGICK

An extreme horror novella

By

Judith Sonnet

⁂MAGICK⁂

For

Carlo Maria Cordio

For crafting the scores that I most often write to.

Absurd, Pieces, Zombie 5: The Killing Birds, Beyond the Door III, Witchery, Beyond Darkness, Deep Blood, Troll 2, Hitcher In the Dark, and Touch of Death are all elevated by your musical madness!

⁂MAGICK⁂

※**MAGICK**※

Other Books by Judith Sonnet:

We Have Summoned

Cabin Possessions

Repugnant

For the Sake Of

Torture the Sinners!

The Clown Hunt

Greta's Fruitcup

Your God Can't Save You

For the Sake Of (2)

Chainsaw Hooker

Something Akin to Revulsion

Low Blasphemy

No One Rides For Free

✶✶**MAGICK**✶✶

THIS BOOK IS RATED

∗∗MAGICK∗∗

CHAPTER ONE.
A HOUSE OF ILL REPUTE

1933

They plied him with alcohol to get him to talk. He spoke in a muffled slur, his words aggravated by the drinks he had consumed and the years he had lived. He was a rough man, coarse haired, thick skinned, and prone to prejudice. In many ways, he was the typical idea of an average American man, and Salt couldn't stand his odorous sweat.

⁘MAGICK⁘

Salt listened intently, trying her best not to chew on her lower lip as the man spoke—his name was Daniel Horton—of ghosts and spirits, and most importantly of the Dobbsin house.

"They calt it a house o' ill repute!" Daniel chuffed. "B-but that ain't even the half of it! The place is damned, I tell ya! Damned!"

Salt's partner was a stoic man named Darren. A tanned man with long, coiled hair and stern eyes. He appeared to listen intently to Daniel, but Salt could tell that Darren's mind was elsewhere. Unlike her, Darren had actually been inside the Dobbsin house. Maybe he knew that there was some truth to what Daniel was saying. Salt was sure that the drunkard was exaggerating, or maybe just exacerbated by booze, but when Darren took something seriously, she felt it was her duty to pay attention.

The three psychics were sitting in the tavern at the outskirts of Baylor, Missouri. The backwoods town was full of hicks, migrants, and destitute soldiers still reeling from the war. Darren was local, but Salt and her similarly gifted husband—Frank—had come from California, where they made their fortune hosting seances for the social elites. They had been summoned by Darren to Missouri. He had requested that they come and explore the Dobbsin house, to ascertain the legitimacy to the claims that it was truly haunted.

✦MAGICK✦

Frank spoke first: "Do you mean to tell us that the Dobbsin house is a brothel?"

Daniel nodded, looking toward Salt and blushing. Even in his drunken state, he didn't want to offend her. She knew it was only because she was beautiful, blonde, and buxom. If she was a wrinkled old fortune teller, he wouldn't even hesitate to fart in her presence.

"Ah-Yuh. That's what I'm sayin'." Daniel stated.

Frank—gray-faced and white-haired—leaned forward and said: "You can speak freely, Mr. Horton. My wife and I are psychics. Do you know what that means? We can commune with the spiritual world, and we seek knowledge in all things. We cannot and will not judge or mock you for what you may or may not have seen in that house. You can tell it to us—all of it—and you will be believed."

Daniel sipped his beer and glanced over his shoulder. The tavern was nearly empty, like the last hour of a funeral. He turned back and said: "It's just that I don't think you three will be da only ones listenin' to whatever tale I tell."

"If it's easier, we have a room upstairs we can take you to." Salt said, trying to be both coy and alluring at once. "You can tell us everything there."

Daniel nodded grimly. "I'd speak my mind more freely, if I was sure I was in the right company."

∴MAGICK∴

Darren led the way, guiding the three pale folks up the stairs and into the room. Salt, and Frank, had only spent a few minutes in the gnarly bedroom before being rushed to Darren's hub. Now that she had a chance to look around, Salt wondered if they shouldn't have asked Darren if he had a guest room. The bed was musty, the window was cloudy, and she could see that the wallpaper was peeling like sunburned skin.

Darren had shown Salt and Frank the records of testimonials, witnesses, and happenings that he had composed. If he was truthful in his findings, then the Dobbsin house had the potential of being declared the most 'charged' building in all of America. It seemed as if something bizarre and uncanny was stirring there on an almost daily basis.

Darren had taken the couple into his study and had shown them a bookshelf, stuffed with leather bound tomes.

"Each one of these is a document of occurrences." Darren said as he pulled a random book loose. "I've been interviewing everyone and anyone I can, and those who are willing to talk have quite a few stories to tell. The problem is that no one in any position of power believes them. Most of these witnesses are outcasts, children, or considered—well–considered likely to fib for attention. But—and you have to take my word on this—I've seen the truth in their eyes and in their voices. They tremor when they talk of this place. I went over and felt that same icy prickle they describe. It is, in my opinion, true that the Dobbsin house is haunted. More so than any other haunt on record! The place... is teeming with supernatural forces."

Salt had been excited to see the Dobbsin house herself. The image of her head was of a gothic mansion, sprawling and vast. A huge palace that leaked white mist and energized those who approached it. Darren seemed intent to make her wait, like an abstinent lover building up to a rapturous wedding night!

She had been a psychic all her life, and so rarely did she feel anything other than a slight pull, but every time the name 'Dobbsin' was spoken, she felt a yank in the pit of her gut. It stirred her up, drew her breath short, and even had an unexpected effect that she had yet to reveal even to her husband. Hearing of the house drew moisture from between her legs. She didn't know why or how, but her sex was slicked with greasy fluid just at the thought of the old, dark place.

There has to be something to these claims if my physical reactions are so insistent and instant. There just has to be! Salt thought as she flipped through Darren's records, biting her lower lip and squeezing her wettened thighs together.

She read many testaments that day.

All of them were weird in nature.

A young boy had seen a nude woman standing at a window, only instead of breasts her chest was adorned with hollowed human heads, with empty eye sockets and toothless mouths. The boy insisted that the peculiar woman had waved at him, and all three of her mouths had smiled at once. Even the mouth attached to her womanly face was as toothless as those affixed to her breasts!

A woman that had recently suffered a miscarriage was lulled into the Dobbsin house at the biding of a baby's mewling cries. Once inside the house, the door swung closed and latched behind her, and the cries turned into an old man's rattling laugh. She stated that she had to kick the door to get it to open, and she looked over her shoulder as she left. She saw an elderly man *crawling* down the stairs and toward her before she raced away from the house and back to her own! Worst of all, the man apparently had the face of a baby. An overly large face, but unmistakably smooth, round, bald, and red from wailing.

How ghastly!

There were other such accounts of odd sightings, close encounters, and terrifying occurrences. The house was so active, it may as well have served dinner along with its constant shows!

Darren asserted that no one had a clearer tale than Daniel Horton, and that they should hear it from his mouth rather than from one of Darren's many books.

They wandered into their room, and everyone found a comfortable place to sit. Daniel rested his rear on the foot of the bed and held his hands nervously at his chest.

"You may speak freely, Mr. Horton." Frank said.

"Go on." Darren stated stoutly.

Daniel nodded and glanced again at Salt. "I-it's a nasty story. Are you sure you wanna hear it, ma'am?"

Already slicked with lubricating juices and itching to relieve herself with her fingers, Salt maintained a composed expression. Her clitoris felt like an almond stuffed down her underclothes.

"I promise you, Mr. Horton, you won't shock me."

Daniel sucked in a breath before unloading his burden:

"It was a whore house back in the day. Dobbsin himself was a mysterious character, so I've heard. He was a pimp of sorts, I believe. Operated the house like a matron. 'til one day he musta had enough of it, because he kilt all of them poor girls. This was in the early 1870's, I think." He looked to Darren, and the man confirmed Daniel's suspicions with a nod. Confident that he had his facts straight, Daniel continued:

"So, he kilt his girls.. And not in no easy way neither. He tied them up, cut them all over, and then drove nails into their heads and... well, the way the story goes, those that survived the nailin' he put to task. He burned them, skinned them, and hung them up in the main lobby by their ankles. Then he kilt himself. Swallowed a bullet. Not 'fore he raped them, of course. Not their livin' bodies, mind you. He raped 'em cold. Mr. Dobbsin, he was an infamous bastard. People came from all over to look at the house where thirteen harlots was butchered. The hauntings, they started shortly after his death. People say and see all sorts of wild and wicked things about the Dobbsin house. But... I didn't believe it 'til a couple years back. That's actually more than a couple years. I was in my teens when it happened. I was just a kid, and me and my pal Liam wanted to..." He trailed off, going red. 'We weren't gonna go to war and die virgins, you see? So, we decided to hustle up a few prostitutes and take 'em somewhere special to... you know... have 'em."

"It's perfectly understandable, sir. You don't have to feel ashamed for such things." Salt said, speaking like a concerned mother lulling a secret from her child's mouth.

Daniel grinned. "Well, we couldn't very well take girls like *that* to our houses. Not with our parents and grandparents around. And if we took 'em to a hotel, then we'd have been spied by some tattletale. So, Liam and I decided to fetch 'em from out of town and take 'em to the Dobbsin house. Neither of us believed in ghosts, but both of us knew the legends. So, we was confident we wouldn't get caught since folks tended to avoid the ol' place." He wiped his brow. "I wish we'd never thought of such a thing. But that's how it happened that we broke in, all giggles and excitement. We had two girls with us, and I'm ashamed to say I don't remember their names. They was pretty, and young. We were giddy, we were. We kept huggin' them and squeezin' them, and they just smiled up at us like we was prince charming! Upon entering the house, our feelings of—erm—elation were amplified. You said I can be honest, right?"

"Right." Salt confirmed.

Daniel nodded as he said: "I have never before or since had a stiffer like the one I got the moment I set foot in that house. I felt like I was gonna explode right in my pants, I did. And it hurt too, like a metal rod had been put right down the middle of my organ!"

There was an awkward beat of silence.

"I tolt you, it's a nasty story." Daniel looked ashamed. "Anyways, I was dying to get myself off, so I wound up draggin' my girl into the first room I could find. I got to work, pulling her clothes off and having her touch me. In no time at all, I was spurting up all over her. She only grazed my dick, and I was already cummin' a fat load! But my cock... it didn't even wilt... and even though I was drippin' spunk I was raring to plow her fields—so to speak."

So, I'm not the only one feeling a sexual reaction to the Dobbsin house. Salt thought. *I wonder if my husband is feeling the same way. Or Darren.*

The thought occurred to her that she could very well be walking into an orgy. If the house had such effects on male potency, what would happen when Frank, Darren, and Salt stepped inside it? Would they fall upon each other?

She imagined watching her husband slicken Darren's shaft with his mouth, all while she lay beneath their host and suckled at his wrinkled scrotum—

"I was inside her when I heard Liam scream." Daniel said, cutting through Salt's vivid fantasies.

"What did you do?" Salt asked.

"I'm real partial not to tell this part of the tale." Daniel said. "But you want the truth? I kept screwin' my girl. She was squirming under me and asking if we better check on Liam and her friend, but I was unstoppable. I pounded her like an animal, cumming up in her cranny even when she tolt me she wanted to leave the house. Then, I..." Daniel stopped. "I kept going, even after I was done. I fucked her three times right in a row before she scrambled out from under me and ran off. I chased her out the door and tried to catch her, my dick still heavy and dripping. I was like a machine... but I stopped in the lobby when I caught sight of what had become of Liam and his girl. At this point, the screaming had stopped." Daniel's face went white, as if he was reliving it. "There wasn't nothing left to scream *with*."

"What do you mean?" Frank asked.

"I mean, the house kilt him. And his girl. They were both hanging upside down by metal hooks. Like, meat hooks you'd see in a butcher's shop, you know. They'd been gutted, their throats had been slit, and their faces were caved in. They was all red, and messy." Daniel stuttered: "a-and the kille-er was still th-there."

"Sorry?" Frank leaned in, hoping for clarification.

Daniel wiped his brow again. It was greased with sweat. Salt also noticed he was pitching a tent in the front of his pants. Even now, the house laid claim on his cock, inflating it by memory alone. Even though this memory was a horrible one, tainted with depravity and violence.

"The killer hadn't left the house. It was standing there, waiting for me to see what it had done ta my best friend. It was-wasn't human." Daniel stated. "It was a d-demon that kilt them both!"

"A demon?" Frank inquired, rubbing his chin.

"Y-yes. Not a ghost. Not a spirit. A demon. An actual demon. And they don't look like they do in the church-books. No red skin, or horns, or tail. The demon was standing between the corpses, and h-he was naked and… and terrible." Daniel seemed unable to offer any description of the demon's appearance. Salt pictured something shadowy and monstrous.

"He spoke to me while I was staring at my dead pal and his dead girl. The demon said—and I'll never forget it—he said: 'Ode to me… the master of suffering. Sing to me… the Lord of Coprophilia'!" Daniel shut his eyes. "Then, he got in a squatting position… and began to drop feces on the floor. He was smiling the whole time too, as if he was happy with the mess he was making. Afterwards, he scooped up his filth, and began to paint Liam's face with it."

Salt swallowed. Why was such a morbid story exciting her? If she so much as breathed the wrong way, she knew an orgasm would rock her body! She tried to focus on Daniel's ugly, wart spackled face, but even that image was further ailing her sodden crotch!

"I ran out. I never saw that girl I… molested. I know the house made me do it, though. Liam's body was never found. I went to war and let me tell you… it was more peaceful than that night had been in the Dobbsin house.

In fact, I preferred it to that horrible, awful, terrible night."

Darren spoke first: "Mr. Horton, I'd like to thank you for your candor." He shook the man's sweaty hand. "You've been a massive help to us and our investigation."

Daniel beamed and said: "Listen, I'm just thankful to get it all out in the open. The whole sordid thing." He looked from one face to another. "Do you believe it?"

"For what it's worth, yes." Frank said. "I don't always take men at their word, but for some reason I'm inclined to under these circumstances."

So, Frank does feel it! The sexual energy of the house is affecting him as much as me! Salt assumed. *We have to go to the Dobbsin house... we have to go tonight...*

⁂

"Tonight?" Frank gulped after Salt told him what she wanted to do.

"Yes. Immediately. I don't know if you meant it or not, but I was convinced by that terrible story. I truly believe that something is going on in the Dobbsin house, and I'd rather confront it now than later." Salt said.

Darren cut in: "Whoa, you don't wanna go at night! That's when it's most active. I don't even go in there when it's dark out!"

"And think of all the first-hand accounts you could write if you did!" Salt proclaimed. "Don't you want to validate all these stories you've recorded?"

Darren shook his head. "The place is a hotbed of violence, evil, and wickedness. Some say that Dobbsin invited the devil as a patron, and that's why he sacrificed his women! Some say—"

"We need to go in. We need to investigate it ourselves, Darren." Salt continued. "And I insist that we do so now. Now that it's dark, and now that whatever is in it will be..." What was the word she was looking for? 'Awake'? 'Active'? She didn't know. "Besides, we can all feel it, can't we?"

"W-what do you mean?" Frank asked.

"Jesus Christ. Okay, I'll say it since you both are scared to. Both of you are stiffer than boards!"

The men blushed, their faces turning as scarlet as a love apple. Darren crossed his legs, trying to conceal the imprint of his burden.

"T-that doesn't mean anything." Frank said. "I mean, what does it prove that we're excited?"

"It's unlike regular excitement, isn't it? It's electric. It's like a beckoning. As if we're all being directed by something. Like puppets. Like..."

"Like our organs are possessed." Darren said. 'All the more reason not to go into that house. You heard Daniel's story. He couldn't control his own desires inside it! What makes you think we'd be any better?"

Because I want it. Salt thought. She pictured again the image of her and her husband interacting with Darren. She imagined the salty taste of his sweaty scrotum as her mouth enveloped it. She imagined tonguing his sheathed testes and listening to him whimper as he ejaculated up and onto Frank's trembling, white stomach. *Yes. I want it. I want to fuck and be fucked in that house. If it doesn't happen, I'll go insane. I'll lose my mind, and I'll blame and hate Frank. I'll wish him dead if he doesn't take me there.*

"We must go to the Dobbsin house." She insisted. "We must!"

Frank shook his head and frowned. "We'll go tomorrow, in the daytime."

"No!" Salt stood and stamped her foot like a tempestuous child. "Absolutely not, you pig!" *Where had that come from?* She was just as shocked by her outburst as the men were. Chastened, Salt looked down at her feet with a frown.

"We'll go... tomorrow." Frank stated, solemnly. "If we go at all."

Frank woke up at night and realized he shouldn't have been surprised to see Salt's side of the bed was empty. Worriedly, he investigated the bathroom and found it vacant. He couldn't imagine she had gone for a stroll, or that she was down at the tavern having a late night drink. He knew exactly where his wife had gone.

To that damned place. The Dobbsin house. My god! Frank threw on his clothes and rushed out of his room. The clock in the hallway told him it was three in the morning. How long had his wife been gone? He felt stupid for having gone so peacefully to sleep, especially after her display in front of Darren. What was worse, Frank still had an erection! It was beginning to hurt too!

Being a medium and a professional occultist, he knew many things about the 'nature' of the unnatural. One thing he and Salt had observed was that in especially charged locations, people didn't act logically. They did, said, and wanted things that made little to no sense to them or those around them. To be a professional, Frank and Salt had fortified their most logical organ, and they never did things without first discussing them with their partners. Well, there was a first time for everything, and Salt's abandonment of Frank felt like a betrayal; as if he had caught her with another man.

The house is drawing her. It's drawing you in too.

Using his quivering prick as a dowsing rod, Frank followed the call of the Dobbsin house. In a matter of minutes, he was stamping down a gravel road and toward the outskirts of Baylor.

No one drove or walked by. It was as if the community had been chomped away by a hungry mouth, leaving Frank on his own. He crossed his arms and shivered, wishing that he hadn't forgotten to grab his jacket before evacuating his room.

Had he even closed the door, or had he left it yawning open? Logic had flown out the window, and Frank was being controlled by his own impulses. He hadn't even thought to scan the tavern for Salt. He hadn't thought to call Darren and see if he was somehow aware of Salt's location. Instead, he had charged out the Inn and raced toward the edge of town, following his cock like a dog on a leash.

Frank blinked, and it was as if his body was transported from the road to a filthy yard. He looked behind him, wondering how he had traveled just so fast! Baylor had become nothing more than a distant glow.

Turning back, Frank felt his jaw drop. He was standing outside the Dobbsin house, and it was terrible to look upon.

The building was made of stone, and it was geometrically perfect. The sides and the roof were equally flat, and the windows were all circular—like the port holes that littered the sides of ships.

The moon reflected off the surface of the three-story building, causing it to shimmer eerily.

Holy God. Jesus Christ, my Savior. Save us.

The door was open, and Frank could hear voices coming from the interior. A low muttering that reminded him of the observations of a loony in an asylum. He heard fragmented words in a language he did not know, but it sounded like Greek.

Frank strode toward the house, despite his desire to turn and run. He wanted to crawl under his covers and pull them over his head and hide like a child, were he allowed to. Frank's free will had been sucked from him. Like a puppet at the whim of a vile puppeteer, Frank moved without his consent.

Frank pulled his shirt over his head and tossed it aside. By the time he stepped through the precipice and into the house, he was shuffling out of his pants.

The inside of the house was cold and damp, but this did not diminish his erection. His balls felt so swollen, he imagined they could be milked like a cow's udders. His nipples stood sturdy, and he clenched his sphincter as if anticipating an unwanted intrusion.

He heard Salt's voice rise from the parlor. She was speaking in a husky whisper, and yet her voice seemed to fill every corner of the main lobby.

"Come... here..." She rasped.

Frank followed the voice, wandering from the lobby and into the parlor.

He screamed at what he saw.

Darren was with her, and they were naked. Only, Darren was no longer breathing. He had been murdered in a most terrible manner.

He was lying on the ground, spread-eagle and stretched out. His pelvis had been broken so that his legs could be cracked open further than allowed. His anus had been plundered with a knobby cane, about the length of an arm. Salt was clasping the shaft of the offensive staff, and she stirred it rapidly, as if churning butter.

Frank could *hear* what the staff was doing to Darren's organs. It was mashing them into a pulp. Pink liquids flowed out from his prolapsed anus whenever the staff was lifted up. The smearing stain was growing between his opened legs like water from a leaking bath.

Darren's face was twisted with pain. His eyes had been gouged out and were hanging by red tendrils down his cheeks. Each eye had been squeezed flat, and their gelled juices decorated him like ejaculate on the face of a whore.

"Oh, God! What have you done?" Frank gasped and held his hands up to his mouth. "What have you done?"

Salt looked up at him with a devilish grin. She spoke in a low tone, which he had never heard her use before: "I want to fuck you forever, Frank. I want to fuck you until there's nothing left."

Frank turned to run but was overwhelmed by a crowd of nude ghosts which had snuck up behind him. They were mutilated, bloodied, and roaring with passionate anger. Each one held their serrated claws out to catch Frank.

He fell into them with a violent scream.

CHAPTER TWO

MAGICK MANOR

2022

Arriving at the Dobbsin house, Jace felt her heartbeat quicken in her chest. She also felt her penis stir in her bikini-thong, hidden underneath her jeans. Yes, it was true what they said, upon approaching the house, one's sexual devices were heightened and intensified. Every time she came to the Dobbsin house, her member would enlarge, and she often had to attend to it vigorously in one of the bathrooms. Sometimes, she didn't make it that far and would instead have to masturbate into one of the many clay pots left in the hallways. They were spittoons, she assumed, but they serviced her better as receptacles for her sperm. It was as if the house demanded an offering in fluids simply for the privilege of being inside it.

Jace unbuttoned, pulling her penis out and rubbing it as she strode through the entrance and ambled down the hall. In a matter of seconds, her sensitive erection was spurting a hot dollop, and barely made it into one of the clay pots, which sat stoutly by the doorframe.

God, this place is wild! Jace Finley thought as she tucked her cock back into her pants and pulled her zipper up.

Jace was tall, smooth skinned, Black, and her hair was dyed a bright red and cut short. She had owned the Dobbsin property for only a few years and was still unfamiliar with its proclivities. Granted, by now it was a quieter place than it had been. She had read the records of Darren Armstrong before he—along with Salt and Frank Mortimer—went missing in 1933. The three psychics had come to explore the house and confirm whether its legends were true. They had gone in at night and had never returned. Since then, the house had become a hotbed for psychic experimentation and exploration. Mediums, charlatans, religious leaders, and even magicians came here from all over the world to test whether or not the stories were true.

For what it mattered, Jace believed every tall tale and urban legend surrounding Dobbsin. The house was absolutely stuffed with energy, and it manifested as sexual potency to *all* who approached it.

Which was why, of course, she had bought the place. Jace was hoping to shoot a pornographic film here, and she wanted to use the houses notoriety as a selling point.

Shot in the sexiest haunted house in America! Cum and see what spirits await!

It was a sleazy tactic, especially since so many people had apparently died in this place, including thirteen prostitutes in the 1800's, but Jace wanted to make a film for a special audience. An audience that cared about spectacle, innovation, and gimmicks.

Jace had made a name for herself as a *real* director in the adult entertainment industry. She didn't just record meat as it slapped against meat. Jace didn't film easy parodies of popular properties. She made films that had heart, character, and soul, as well as consistent and beautiful fucking.

Jace even had a title worked out already. Her new film would be called *MAGICK MANOR*. She had done her research, and the moniker had been used to describe the brothel back in its heyday. Back before the house had been tarnished by oddities and murder.

Jace had wanted to utilize the house the moment she learned about it via a true crime documentary she had streamed on Netflix. The documentary was bawdy and had taken off among young audiences, who were shocked by its startling content. Striking while the iron of inspiration was hot, Jace had reached out to the filmmakers and through them found out that the property had been inherited by a long distant relative of Henry Dobbsin, the notorious whore-killer himself! The older woman had let the house fall into decrepitude, and it was all too easy to pry her away from her deed with a few thousand dollars. Their entire interaction had been over the phone, and the old woman left Jace with a warning:

"It ain't hokum. The place is... it's evil."

Jace nodded into her phone before saying: "I'll be careful."

She wasn't so sure she had believed it back then, but now, she had no choice. Jace had been renting a room in Baylor–above a historic old tavern—and had witnessed terrible things on the property.

The Dobbsin house was hard to define. It wasn't a castle, a manor, or a mansion, but it wasn't a normal house. It was tall and its walls were gray and made from stone. It was almost featureless, without many windows and doors. The roof was flat too, meaning that water pooled over the house's top on wet days. It looked like a magnificent cube. Three stories tall and narrow.

Someone had spray painted the words 'MAGICK MANOR' over the doorway in black. They had added two sets of three stars by either side of the first word.

Jace had already been through the house with her video camera, taking pictures and steady clips of every nook and cranny she could find. The house was surprisingly clean despite being abandoned and uncared for. There were cobwebs aplenty, which she had swept up with a broom and dustpan purchased from a local Dollar-Mart.

If there are ghosts in Magick Manor, then maybe they're good housekeepers.

The rooms were all featureless and dark with the air inside the place was wet and chilly. Each room felt conductive, as if an electric energy was pulsating from the walls.

The first ghost Jace had seen had been out from the corner of her eye. She had been walking down the hallway with a camera when she walked by a room with an opened door. She caught a flash of movement, which caused her heart to jolt and made her skid to a stop. Jace froze, then swiveled in place and directed her camera into the room.

✶✶MAGICK✶✶

A woman was sitting cross-legged on the floor. She was nude, young, and beautiful. Her eyes were closed, and her lips were held tightly together, as if she was scared to breathe.

"Hello?" Jace asked, stepping into the doorway and adjusting the focus on her video camera.

The woman said nothing. Her strawberry hair stirred, as if a gust of wind had somehow slipped through the impenetrable walls. An invisible hand took hold of her hair and lifted it like a leash. The girl cracked her head back and her lips came unsealed. Jace gasped as she watched the girl's throat open up like a secondary mouth beneath her chin.

Instead of blood, a black ink sputtered out of the wound with an arid hiss. The goo splattered across the flat cold cement floor, landing mere inches away from the toes of Jace's sneakers.

As she leapt back the girl seemed to dematerialize. She faded into her environment, her skin turning icy and gray and her hair going bone–white before paling into dust. Then she was gone. Totally gone. Not even her blotted fluids remained on the floor. It was as if the dark room had swallowed her up and licked its plate clean afterwards.

Jace reviewed the video footage and was relieved to see she had captured the incident on camera. Of course, she should have sent the footage to the documentary crew that had filmed in the house previously. Aside from a few weird noises and glowing orbs, they hadn't managed to catch anything confirming the paranormal nature of the Dobbsin house. All they could do was speculate over whether or not the legends were true.

Jace had only been in the house a few times before gleaning irrefutable evidence that not only were ghosts real, but they were active in Magick Manor.

She should have sent the video to someone—anyone—but she didn't. She was still confused as to why that was. The house seemed to hold some influence over Jace's thinking—beyond what it did to her groin every time she neared it—but she didn't want to *share* her findings. She began to theorize that maybe the documentary crew had caught unquestionable evidence of the supernatural, but they too had been unwilling to divulge their truths with the common public. The house, like a cloistered nun, had its secrets, and only a special few were privy to them.

Jace felt privileged, as if the house was showing itself naked to her, preparing for her to take its virginity.

She felt her cock rise again, even though Jace had just masturbated into one of the houses many receptacles.

Another pound of flesh... or spunk. Whatever. The house needs a sacrifice, and I need relief.

Jace lowered her trousers down to her knees and let her thong hang like a hammock between her thighs. She licked her palm before rubbing her throbbing cock. She waddled as she masturbated until she found a clay pot sitting beneath an oval window in what could have been a parlor. Looking out the window and across the overgrown lawn, Jace caught sight of a van climbing a hill and dancing toward the house. The sun glinted sharply from the vehicle as it approached.

Jace smiled, knowing that her cast, and her small crew were moments away. They had all been warned of the house and its effects on the human body, but she doubted any of them had taken her warnings seriously.

"Really," she had said over the phone, "this place is like instant Viagra."

"Sure. Sure. So, you have a script?" Geoff asked.

"Yes. It's written up already. I just need a skeleton crew for this one. You, Daisey, Kayla, and Swann, if he's free."

"Swann's definitely free." Geoff had said. "I just spoke to him yesterday and he's itching for work."

"Good. Tell him to bring his A-game. This place is a fountain of inspiration!"

"Whatever you say, Jace." Geoff sounded unenthused.

I bet his prick is bursting now. Jace thought, smiling devilishly as she imagined warm pussies and hard dicks. She ejaculated, missing the pot and staining the stone wall. Her seed dropped down in snotty strands, inching toward the floor in a slow crawl.

Jace yanked up her pants after squeezing out the last droplets of sperm from her swollen and raw organ. Then, she reached down and scooped up her offering with a finger and deposited it into the pot.

Magick Manor seemed to shudder around her, as if it was expressing its own pleasure at what she had just done.

There'll be more where that came from, you greedy thing. Jace thought. *You just wait and see...*

CHAPTER THREE
SWANN SONG

Swann's mind was ailing with depravity.

Of course, no one else in the van knew of such things. He kept his lecherous atrocities to himself and had managed to skirt away from the consequences of his actions for a decade. Now, while approaching the house, Swann couldn't help but feel his baser urges reclaiming his mind. He looked at Daisey and wished he could batter her face into a pulp, and then fuck its center. He looked at Kayla and wanted to use a cheese grater to shred her pussy apart, and then he wanted to pull the mangled meat away in strands, sucking them into his mouth like wet spaghetti noodles and—

Christ! Get a hold of yourself! Swann thought with a shudder. He realized that Jace's warning had been correct. The house amplified one's sexual needs as one approached it. The problem was only that Swann's sexual desires were of a deviant nature—and not the sort that was accepted as 'kink' in modern society. His were barbaric, ruthless, and primal. When Swann was working, it was merely a task that must be performed. His erections and ejaculations were all just a part of the job. He would never admit it, but he felt *nothing* when he was on camera—even though he was so often fucking some of the most beautiful girls in the industry. Take Kayla and Daisey for example.

Daisey Dabney was tall, slender, and her hair was cut short and dyed black. With a magnificent chest, coltish legs, and a smile that men ached to cum upon, she was an award winner—and a class act to boot!

Kayla Roth was dark haired, curvy, and was well known for partaking in kinkier videos. Currently, she was wearing a pair of overalls and nothing else. Her tits jiggled as the van mounted the gravel road leading toward the Dobbsin house.

While most men—and women—would have been entranced by such a voluptuous sight, Swann wanted nothing more than to use a cigar cutter to detach her nipples from her breasts so he could force her to swallow them—

Stop it, stop it, stop it!

Swann felt an erection blossom in his pants. It was a true one, not the erections he designed for his work. This stiffened organ was pumping with the kind of lust he only felt at the sight and smell of blood.

How long has it been since you last got off, Swann? Truly?

It had been exactly three weeks.

Swann had chosen his victim at a bar. He followed her home, snuck in through the window, and pounced upon her bed. She had struggled against him, wanting to scream but unable to as he stuffed a sock into her mouth.

Oh, the things he had done to her.

Swann smiled, recalling just how easy it had been to use a knife to unzip her belly. He recalled how much her organs had jiggled as he continued to fuck her dying corpse.

He had broken her open so far that he could look into the bowl of her pelvis and watch as his cock entered and exited her bloodied cunt—

You're a freak. An animal. A monster.

"You feel it too, right?" Kayla asked, breaking Swann from his revere. "It's exactly like Jace said! I'm wetter than... Christ! I'm wetter than I think I've ever been!"

"I'm glad you said it first." Geoff said from the front seat. The portly crewman turned and looked into the back of the van. His face was sweaty, and his sunglasses did little to hide his excitement. "I swear, I haven't felt this hard since I was a teenager!"

Daisey shrugged. "It's just the idea of it that's doing this to us. Like a placebo. We all thought it would happen, so it's a self-fulfilling prophecy, isn't it?"

"I dunno. I think Jace may have been right. We're almost there, and I was actually thinking about baseball until I caught sight of that place." Geoff pointed out the windshield. "Now, I just want to beat off as soon as possible!"

Daisey looked toward Swann. "Are you feeling it too? If not, that disproves the whole thing."

"No. I... I feel it." Swann confirmed with a grin.

"I'm glad my tits are already out." Kayla murmured, tweezing one of her browned nipples.

God, if you only knew how much I wanted to hurt you. Swann looked down at the floor and away from his co-star. They'd be fucking soon enough, but it wouldn't be real for him. Not without blood, and panic. Not without screaming, and weeping, and begging...

He had fucked the last girl for hours, even after she had gone cold.

CHAPTER FOUR
A SORDID HISTORY

The house was in the middle of nowhere, and so Jace was certain that her crew and cast would feel liberated upon entering the peculiar abode. Instead, they became reserved; even Kayla covered her breasts with her hands upon walking in.

"This place really is creepy." Kayla said with a tremble. "Like a giant prison cell!"

"It's not that bad." Jace said, suddenly finding herself defensive of Magick Manor. She shook her head and put her hands against her hips.

"You were right about its—erm—effects." Geoff said, adjusting his cargo shorts. Geoff was heavyset, bearded, and red-haired. He was a brilliant camera man, and he had brought a digital 4K device with him which he was already setting atop a sturdy tripod. Their productions raked in enough cash they could probably afford movie quality equipment, but Jace and Geoff stayed afloat through frugality. They didn't spare any expenses on sound equipment though, and Jace would be holding up a fuzzy-headed microphone as well as directing.

"Any lines we need to memorize?" Swann asked, stretching his arms over his head. His shirt lifted, exposing his washboard stomach. Blonde-haired, blue-eyed, and strong-armed, Swann was one of the only men Jace had ever felt any inkling of attraction toward. He also had a reputation for being one of the kindest and nicest men working in porn. Some called him the "Keanu Reeves of Adult Entertainment" due to his compassionate attitude. He was modest as well, so much so that he seemed uninterested in bedding *any* of his co-stars off camera.

"This will be more of a visual piece for now." Jace said. "A little artsy, maybe a little scary, but *very* sexy." She hesitated before adding: "I don't want to just shoot the one movie here. I kind of bought this place and figured we could use it as a studio after a while."

"Really?" Daisey lifted her brows.

Jace actually hadn't thought such a thing until this very moment. She attributed the idea to the house and the preternatural urges, and yet she couldn't argue herself away from the idea. She wanted to never leave this place. It was like a drug, a constant aphrodisiac that controlled her willpower and directed her as if she was a player on a board.

"You really want to relocate everything to... Missouri?" Geoff's eyes had gone wide. He lived in Chicago and had probably assumed this road trip was a one time thing. Jace realized she hadn't revealed that she had bought Magick Manor, only that they were using it for the one film. She decided to tell them later, instead opting to give them a smile and say:

"It's just an idea. Anyways, let's get to work, yeah? Scripts are sitting in the parlor. Go and give 'em a read."

The cast wandered away from the lobby and into a sparse parlor, where Jace had left a small stack of papers upon an empty bar. The script had been written in a flurry, and she attested that to Magick Manor's influence as well.

✦MAGICK✦

Separated from the cast, Geoff spoke up: "You okay, Jace? We haven't heard from you in a while, and—"

"I'm fine. Just spent some time scouting out locations here." Jace didn't want to tell him she had been recording ghosts and paranormal activity. She now had twenty-three examples of Magick Manor's supernatural inhabitants, starting with the girl whose throat had been cut by an invisible foe.

Geoff paused before saying: "I watched the documentary about this place after you told me about it."

"What did you think?"

"It honestly scared me knowing you were here on your own." Geoff said. "I mean, I don't believe in ghosts or nothing—" *You will.* Jace thought. "—but this place has one helluva history behind it. I mean, the guy it's named after killed thirteen prostitutes. Th-that ain't even the worst of it! Did you know that in the 1960's a serial killer squatted here for a week? He abducted, raped, and *ate* five children! Children!" Geoff released a gust of exasperated air. "I just don't think it's appropriate for us to be... filming a fuck flick in a place where stuff like *that* happened."

Jace felt an icy prickle of fear crawl up her sweat-slicked back. Instead of telling Geoff that she agreed, and that she didn't know why she insisted on doing this, she said: "Oh, c'mon, Geoff. You sound like a real pearl-clutcher.

Nothing like that has happened since the 80's, and this place isn't haunted. It's got a sordid past sure, but so do most places in America. Hell, every building is practically haunted these days."

Geoff frowned. "You don't believe that. I can see it in your eyes."

Jace shook her head.

Geoff advanced toward her. "You've seen stuff here, haven't you?"

"I thought you didn't believe in ghosts." Jace whispered.

"I don't, but I think *you* do." Geoff said.

⁎⁎**MAGICK**⁎⁎

CHAPTER FIVE
READING

"God, what is this?" Daisey turned through the pages of her script. She felt weird about the whole venture, but this script was the icing on the cake. As she read, the pressure on her groin intensified, and her eyesight started to blur. It was as if the house itself was molesting her. *Jace must be out of her mind.* She thought with reluctance. Not only was their director hanging out in the weirdest house imaginable, but the script she had written for them to perform was utter and complete nonsense. Usually, Jace's scripts were filled with realistic yet

✦MAGICK✦

alluring dialogue. She had actual plots in her porn flicks, and that's what attracted Daisey to Jace's many projects. Like many girls, she had gone into the industry with hopes of eventually becoming a real actor. Unfortunately, unpaid theater internships, community programs, and auditions didn't pay the bills.

Jace did.

Tech-bros with I-Phones and hard cocks did. Roles in movies like *Pussy Pounders 18: The Fuck-Fest* did.

Jace's films were different from most of the porn Daisey acted in. Jace actually cared about making the bodies on her screen appear human. She didn't give a single damn about smooth makeup or colored lighting; she cared about people having fun and getting off while they were at it!

No woman in a Jace Fingering production was a simpering bimbo that spoke like a child. No man was a rough bastard unless he was *asked* to be. Hell, Jace made as much a deal out of expressed consent as she did the first shot of full penetration!

This script on the other hand, reflected a different artist entirely. One that rambled and didn't know nor care how human beings communicated. It was also rougher than anything Jace had created before.

There was an instance about sticking a massive, knobby cane up someone's ass. There was another part where two people were hung upside down while a third took a shit and rubbed their filth over their victims faces. There was another section where a couple of lovers were made to strangle and kill each other, all while fucking. It felt more like a horror movie than a porno, and Daisey didn't like the sound of that!

"Maybe she printed the wrong script." Kayla offered, flipping through the pages with a repulsed look on her face.

"I think it's pretty hot." Swann said.

"Hardy-har." Daisey laughed.

Swann shrugged and returned to the script.

"I'm going to talk to her, because I'm not filming *this*." Daisey said. "I don't do hardcore kink stuff and I definitely don't do scat! Maybe piss but... not scat."

"Yeah. That's gross." Kayla closed her papers and put them back on the bar-top. "I wish there was some booze leftover. That'd make this place less creepy, if we could get blitzed."

"I could definitely use a drink." Swann mused, mostly to himself. He was so overtly polite it almost annoyed Daisey.

"Did you watch the documentary about Magick Manor?" Daisey asked her costars.

"I did." Swann said. "It's pretty freaky, all the stuff that happened here?"

"Yeah." Kayla muttered. "I started it but after it got to the part about the girl that cut out her own womb I had to stop."

Daisey shuddered. "I don't think I even made it that far. I stopped after they talked about those psychics that vanished in the thirties. The Mortimer's? Frank and Salt?"

"Odd name." Swann said. "Salt Mortimer? Odd name."

"Odd couple." Daisey continued. "They were apparently pretty famous. Like the Ed and Lorraine Warren's of the '30's. Before they went missing while investigating *this* house."

Kayla began to whistle the theme song for *The Twilight Zone*.

"Ugh." Daisey said. "I have to pee. Where's Jace and Geoff."

"You wanna do it on camera?" Kayla looked shocked, even though she had pissed on camera multiple times without shame.

"No, I'd just rather not wander around without knowing where I'm going."

"You could use one of these pots." Swann said, indicating a clay item underneath an oval window. "Although, I think they've already been used."

"What do you mean?" Kayla walked over and peered into the pot. She giggled. "Looks like Jace has been busy! This one's almost full!"

"What? Has she been going to the bathroom in them?" Daisey asked, curious and repulsed.

"No." Swann stated. 'She's been cumming in them!"

"Oh, God!" Kayla laughed. "It's the effects of the Dobbsin house! Potency! Insatiability! I swear, I could cum if someone just breathed on me the right way! I don't blame the girl!"

"I'll pee first and cum later." Daisey joked as she looked around the parlor's exit. She saw Jace and Geoff standing in the lobby, holding a heated discussion in whispers.

"Hullo?" Daisey asked.

Jace turned, her face bleached with red swirls. Apparently, the conversation she and Geoff were having was a testy one. "Hey, love." Jace gathered her composure and gave Daisey a smile.

"Is there a bathroom here?"

"Oh, huh." Jac scratched the back of her head. 'There's no working plumbing or electricity, so I've just been going outside."

"Oh." Daisey frowned, disappointed. "Is there an outhouse or—"

"There's a bathroom of sorts. Kind of just a chute that leads beneath the house—"

"I'll go outside." Daisey smirked and headed toward the door. She was relieved to leave the house. Its atmosphere was cold and oppressive, and Daisey was happy to stand in the languid sun. She turned her head up toward a beam and basked in it.

She almost forgot the pressure on her bladder, but a dull ache brought her back to reality. She walked around toward the side of the house, towed down her pants, and squatted. There was a football field worth of space between her and the dense woods beside the house. The woods were dark, and Daisey imagined shadowy figures standing beneath the trees. Her bladder clenched up with fright, but she was able to convince it to open with a reassuring thought:

There's no one out here. You're all alone, sweetie. Just do your thing and head back in a moment. No one's here—

She began to pee.

I could never do this on camera. I wonder how Kayla does it. Daisey mused as she watched a clear stream trickle between her ankles.

She looked up as the last droplets of urine fell out of her—

--and gasped when she realized she was being watched.

Daisey released a scream.

∴∴MAGICK∴∴

CHAPTER SIX
ARE YOU IN HELL?

Jace chased after Geoff. He had dashed out quickly, holding his camera in one hand and pumping the other. They both followed the sound of Daisey's screams. When they rounded the corner and came to the side of the house, she was hoisting her drawers up, and Jace couldn't help but notice a wet spot blooming across the seat of her clothes.

"What happened?" Geoff asked, striding in front of Daisey and looking toward the woods.

"I saw someone!" Daisey said in a flurry. "They were standing in the woods and... and, oh GOD, there was something wrong with them!"

"What do you mean?" Geoff asked.

"Are they still there?" Jace asked, hoping to hide her excitement from her startled starlet.

With a trembling hand, Daisey pointed toward a narrow aisle of trees. "He was standing right in between those two, and he was... watching me!"

"What was *wrong* with him?" Geoff asked.

Daisey shook her head. "It's—it's crazy. You'll think I'm crazy." She put a hand against her brow.

"Tell me what you saw. Don't worry, we won't call you names." Jace put a reassuring hand on Daisey's shoulder. "You just tell us what you saw."

Daisey swallowed and crossed her arms over her breasts. "He was naked, and he had... he had *lumps*."

"What do you mean? Was he fat?" Geoff asked.

"No. He was skinny. He just had... things growing out of him. Like, massive tumors!" Daisey shuddered. "I don't wanna be here, Jace. This place is scary and weird and... and let's go film somewhere else!"

Jace shook her head. "No, Daisey, I promise you, this place is safe." *Why am I saying that? I know for a fact it isn't. I'm not allowed to tell her she's right, and that what she saw was probably only the first of many.*

✥MAGICK✥

"Maybe you'll feel better inside and out of the sun? You just need some water. Did you drink any during the trip? It was a long drive."

Daisey snarled, turning around and showing her wet ass. "Yes, I drank water, you bitch!"

Jace flinched. Even when Daisey was angry, she never swore. The only time she used dirty words was when she was on camera. She had turned so hateful so fast. Before Jace could respond, Geoff spoke up:

"How about I go look around? If there's some perv out there, we'll kick him out. Then we can all sit down and have a family meeting, okay?"

He glared at Jace.

"And if everyone wants to leave, then we will."

"Fine." Jace clenched her fists by her side.

Geoff started toward the woods.

"Wait!" Jace called out. He turned and watched as Jace approached. "Leave your camera here, okay?" She held out a hand, and Geoff plopped the device into her palm.

Jace and Daisey watched as Geoff trudged toward the woods, his gait slow and steady. The moment he was out of earshot, Daisey whirled on Jace and said:

"What the fuck is that script about?"

"What do you mean?"

"I mean it's the most perverted and ugly shit you've ever done. You never write rough stuff like that!"

"What. Are. You. Talking. About?" Jace enunciated.

"I mean, you have a scene where someone breaks open a woman's jaw and vomits into it. You have a scene where a guy pulls out an eyeball and screws it into an anus. You have—"

"Whoa! What the fuck! I didn't write anything like that!" Jace insisted with raised hands.

Daisey's face was screwed up with confusion. "That's what was in the script."

"No. My script is a simple gothic romance. A bit spooky... but all the sex in it is sweet and consensual. Not violent!"

Daisey chewed on her lower lip. Tears started to flower out of the corners of her eyes. "A-are you joking?"

"No. I swear, I didn't write anything like... *that*."

'Then how'd that end up in the parlor?"

"I don't know. Let's go inside and find out."

The two women started toward the front of the house. Jace looked over her shoulder and watched as Geoff broke through the trees and dissipated into the woods. The shadows swallowed him up like candy.

"Jace?" Daisey asked.

"Yes?"

"Do you have an extra pair of pants for me to wear?" She was red-faced.

"Absolutely." Jace said.

∴**MAGICK**∴

CHAPTER SEVEN
BABIES

Geoff wasn't so sure this was a good idea now that he was in the forest, but he couldn't stop himself from following his instincts. He had been driven away from Jace and Daisey, assured by some primordial part of his brain that they were simply women and incapable of handling a situation like this without his guidance—

I didn't take you for a misogynist, Geoff.

He shook his head, hoping the detestable thought would leave him. It stayed latched to his brain, insisting that if he didn't handle this, it would never get handled at all.

The ground between the house and the forest had been flat, but the area behind the trees was sloped and hilly. He careened down a leave-decorated slant and his feet plodded into a mushy mud pile.

Cripes. There go my shoes. He thought as he skidded up an incline and worked his way around a shallow streamlet. It was cold in the woods, just as it had been unexpectedly cold inside the Dobbsin house.

Daisey is right. We shouldn't be here.

He heard a raspy chuckle from behind him.

Geoff turned around and watched as a flash of naked skin vanished behind a knotty tree.

"Hey! Hey, you!" Geoff dashed toward the tree. "This is private property, asshole! C'mon!"

Another laugh resounded through the woods. Geoff heard a snicker of crunching leaves and watched as the naked figure darted out from behind the tree and ducked away from sight. He crawled on all fours, which alarmed Geoff, since the man was more dexterous than he had imagined. Still, Geoff couldn't get a good look at the weirdo. He moved so quickly, all Geoff could perceive was his white flesh and his scuttling limbs, then he was out of sight.

"Hey!" Geoff called, coming around the bush and being surprised that the man was nowhere to be seen. Geoff turned on his heels and scanned the forest. Where had the fucker gone?

"Ah-Ha!" The stranger hooted.

Geoff followed the noise, squeezing between two shrub laden trees and found himself in a sunlit meadow. He saw the crooked end of a wrought iron fence leaning like a shipwreck at the far end of the plot and realized that he had stepped foot into a long-abandoned cemetery. Geoff felt his pulse thud in his ears as he stumbled around the corroded, nameless headstones. They had been beaten in by the weather and by a general lack of attention.

That's a sad thought. When you die, you expect your name to live immortal through your grave, don't you? Well, here's proof that nothing but nothing lasts forever—

He heard the naked man laugh from a distance. The creep sounded like a cartoon character, yuck-yuck-yucking away as if he had just been told a new joke. Geoff realized that he was starting to hate that laugh.

If I get my hands on this bastard, I'll wring his goddamn neck.

Geoff had never felt so angry before. He really did believe that if given the opportunity the eccentric pervert was in danger of being killed. Geoff felt fumes seep between his teeth, as if his insides were heating up with rage.

"Get the fuck out here, right now!" Geoff shouted.

"Huh-huh!" The man laughed, and it was like putting a spark to gasoline.

"You fuckin' *shit*!" Geoff loped toward the end of the graveyard, stomping through the overgrown grass. His foot slammed against a squatting stone. Geoff tumbled over, smashing his head against the ground. His eyes fuzzed over with pain. He pulled the limb up and breathed in deeply, seething with irritation.

"Ha!" The man sputtered before running out of the woods and toward Geoff.

Geoff looked up and couldn't quite believe what he was seeing.

The man was just as Daisey had described. He was emaciated. So skinny that his ribs were imprinted against a thin sheath of translucent skin. His belly was flapping with growths, which reminded Geoff of barnacles and plump fruits. Actually, they reminded Geoff of cow udders!

The man was hairless, his flesh was snow-white, and his eyes were pale. They looked like two gunky moons sitting on his sallow cheeks. The only bits of color he carried were his yellowed teeth and crooked fingernails.

He ran like a dog, dashing across the meadow and toward Geoff.

Geoff scuttled backward, scrambling against the ground for a foothold. The floor of the graveyard was wet and muddy.

"No, no, no!" Geoff stood and ran toward the woods. He looked over his shoulders and saw that the laughing, naked freak was in hot pursuit. The deformed man's cragged smile was unwavering, and his flopping growths swatted the ground beneath him as his legs overtook his arms, then sprang him forward.

"Help!" Geoff called, hoping that someone—anyone—would hear him and come to his aide.

The freak hooted behind him, laughing as if this was merely a game and not the most terrifying event in Geoff's life.

Geoff exited the graveyard and trundled through the woods. Branches clawed at him, and his leg brushed through a thorn bush. The pain couldn't stop him. He had been ignited with adrenaline. All Geoff could think was:

Run! Run! Run! Run! Run!

It was his mantra. His prayer.

Jesus Christ, RUN!

He looked again.

The man was on his hind legs, running like a track star.

⁙MAGICK⁙

Geoff turned back and plowed through the woods, slipping along the side of a creek bed and rolling his ankle. He immediately felt sore, and he could have allowed the injury to floor him, but he put mind over matter and worked through it. Geoff bit into his tongue as he rushed further and further into the woods.

You moron. You're running away from the Dobbsin house! No one will hear you scream when that thing catches you!

Geoff turned a corner and was shocked to see a crypt standing in the center of a circle of saplings. The crypt was decimated by bad weather, and it reminded him more of a porta-potty than it did a resting place.

Geoff would have run past the crypt, except that the door was open, and a figure was standing before it. Illogically, Geoff wondered if the person was there to help him.

He realized that the figure was naked. The specter was also holding his own intestines in his hands, like a bundle of bloody roses.

The disemboweled man smiled toward Geoff and said:

"The devil's going to fuck you, pornographer!"

Geoff felt a huge amount of pressure on his back. The twisted freak had grabbed him from behind and threw him to the ground.

"No! No!" Geoff struggled against the freak as it knelt down over him. He pushed a hand against the freak's face, and his fingers fell into the monstrous man's gaping, yellow-fanged mouth. Without hesitating, the freak bit down on Geoff's digits. They were crunched up like carrots, spouting blood across the freak's too-white face.

Geoff screamed as the freak tore away from his hand, separating him from his ring, index, and middle fingers.

"No! No! No!" Geoff cried as his own blood rained down on his face. The blood was hot and sour, and it tasted like battery acid on his tongue. Geoff began to sputter and cry.

The disemboweled man had vanished. There was no helping Geoff. He was alone with the freak.

The freak took Geoff's head, lifted it, and slammed it back into the moist earth. The motion stunned Geoff, cutting his screams short. Geoff lay on his back, watching in mute terror as the creature squatted over his pelvis and began to rub his abnormal growths. The lumps began to quiver, like jelly on toast. The freak was grinning too, blood leaking between his almond-shaped chompers.

For the first time since Geoff had seen him, the freak spoke. His voice was crystal-clear. It would have been beautiful had it come from someone that *wasn't* covered in blood and pulsating tumors. The freak said:

"It's okay. It'll be over soon."

Then, the freak grabbed a hold one of his tumors and ripped it open. Yellow fluids gushed from the lump as it deflated. The liquid spattered down on Geoff's chest, staining his shirt and icing his flesh. He felt droplets of the rancorous stew land on his tongue. If he had thought his own blood had tasted awful, it was nothing compared to the creature's inner slop. He felt as if someone had just spewed diarrhea into his mouth, and no matter how hard he spluttered the taste refused to leave his tongue.

Geoff watched in terror as a creature fell out from the sac after the fluids had been vacated. The creature looked like a skinned fetus. It was pink and veiny, but undeniably human in form.

The freak moaned in an obscenely orgasmic manner as the newly birthed monster began to crawl up Geoff's chest and toward his screaming maw.

"NO!" Geoff shouted as the creature gripped his lower jaw and pulled it open with unnatural strength. "No!" It was the last intelligible word Geoff was capable of saying before the fetus pushed its head into his jaw. Geoff felt his teeth shatter in his gums, breaking open and tumbling down his throat in shrapnel. Geoff shut his eyes and pushed his tongue against the fetus's bald head. It felt as hard as a stone. It was as if the fetus was made of stone, and it was being crammed down Geoff's oral cavity by an angered wrestler.

Geoff felt and heard his jaw break. It flopped down and lay askew as the fetus wriggled in deeper… and deeper.

Geoff's throat began to bulge unnaturally. His esophagus *crinkled* as the fetus filled it. Geoff screeched and burbled. The fetus's legs stuck out from his bloodied mouth, like a half-buried corpse in Dante's hell. Its little toes wiggled like upturned worms.

Before Geoff died, he heard the freak break open another tumor. Soon, more fetuses were finding different holes to crawl into. He felt them crowding around his already decimated mouth, before one decided to use its nubby fingers to pull one of his eyes loose from its socket. Geoff heard the stringy tendons break inside his skull, and he felt his orbital socket collapse as the baby nudged itself into its void.

He felt the freak pull his trousers down, and Geoff knew—even as he breathed his last—that no part of his body would go unviolated.

✨**MAGICK**✨

CHAPTER EIGHT
CUM DUMPSTER

Jace and Daisey weren't talking about it, but Kayla was certain that something awful had happened outside.

"We'll tell you about it when Geoff gets back." Jace insisted.

Swann yawned and stretched. He seemed to be genuinely disappointed when Jace told him that she had no idea how that disturbing script had replaced the one she had spent several nights writing. It concerned Kayla, but distantly. The truth was, now that she was here, she really wanted to explore the Dobbsin house. It scared her, but she was finding herself drawn toward its inner chambers.

Daisey was reluctant to explore.

"This place is weird." She stated with crossed arms and a frown.

"Okay, but like, I'd rather look around when it's daytime than at night." Kayla said.

"I'd rather not look at all." Daisey turned her nose upward.

"It'll be nighttime soon." Swann said, looking at his wristwatch. "Maybe in about fifteen minutes."

"We should leave before it gets dark out." Daisey said.

"Let's wait for Geoff first, hun." Jace said. "I bet he'll be back any moment now."

Kayla sighed and hefted herself up to her feet. She hooked her fingers through the straps of her overalls and started to walk away from the parlor.

'Where are you going?" Daisey almost shrieked.

"I'm just taking a walk." Kayla said. "Don't have an aneurysm."

"I'll go with you." Swann said. "Just to... you know... keep you safe."

Kayla blushed as the blonde man strode up beside her. The two walked out of the parlor and up the stairs. When they were out of earshot, Kayla asked:

"What do you think happened?"

"With Daisey? I dunno, but she screamed pretty loud!"

"Maybe she saw a ghost." Kayla half joked.

At the top of the stairs, Kayla looked back toward the lobby. Everything in the house was so flat and boring, it looked as if the whole building was filmed in black-and-white. She hoped they'd find something exciting in at least one of the rooms.

Swann took her hand and gave it a gentle squeeze. It was reassuring and polite. "You doing okay?"

"Yeah. A bit confused. I'm also still super horny." Kayla giggled. "Like everyone else here, right?"

"I know what you mean." Swann smirked.

"Do you?" Kayla looked toward the front of his pants. Indeed, his pipe was standing tall. Kayla suddenly wished she had him in her mouth, even though they were far away from Jace and her camera.

A little extracurricular fucking, huh? You've never been about that before. It's the house. It has to be!

"What do you think?" Kayla said as the two investigated a nearby room. It was totally empty and cold, like a newly purchased refrigerator. There was a circular window which overlooked the dismal lawn, but nothing beyond that in terms of decoration. The two turned and walked down the hall, finding another similarly vacant room.

"I think this place is a dump." Swann admitted.

"Me too. I don't know why Jace wants to film here." Kayla bit her lip. "I mean, it's like the blandest haunted house in—"

She opened the nearest door and gasped at what was inside.

"Whoa." Swann said, genuinely impressed.

"D-did Jace do this?" Kayla asked, taking a bouncy step into the room. Unlike the rest of Magick Manor, this room lived up to its name. The walls were obscured behind silky, red curtains, and there was a fluffy bed in the room's center. Leaning against the furthest wall was an X-framed stockade, adorned with leather straps on each corner of its form. Beside it stood a bookshelf littered with multi-colored sex toys: dildos, vibrators, and strings of pearly anal beads.

"This has to be our set!" Swann said, stepping in beside Kayla. "I mean, all of this looks new!"

"Well, I like this way more than anything she put in that horrid script!" Kayla said, observing a leather riding crop. She picked it from the shelf and traced it along the curve of her ass. "Wanna do a practice run?" She asked.

Swann swallowed. "A-are you sure?"

"Yes. C'mon, both of us are fit to burst! Let's mess around a bit before Jace starts directing!" Kayla said with a sly smirk.

Swann scratched the back of his head and looked toward the floor, bashfully.

"Listen, I know you don't fuck your co-stars off camera, but I'm giving you clear consent. I won't '#metoo' you." Kayla chuckled and swiped the riding crop across his nose, playfully.

"It's not that." Swann said. "It's just that I have some fetishes I... I don't tend to talk about."

Kayla raised her brows. "Oh, really?"

"Yeah. I mean, honestly, it's pretty weird. The stuff I like is... outside the norm." He flinched at his own words.

"Mums the word." Kayla unclasped her overalls and shucked her shoulders. The pants fell down revealing a pair of pink panties. Tufts of wiry pubic hair stuck out along the trim of her underclothes. There was a sopping stain on her crotch, which had caused the fabric to draw in and outline the crease of her sex. Kayla hooked her fingers around her panties and drew them down to her knees, then she stood upright so that Swann could observe her nude form. She reached down and parted her fat pussy lips, exposing the velvety skin within.

"A-are you really s-sure?" Swann asked nervously. He unbuttoned, unzipped, and revealed his massive cock. The veins seemed to thump with an electronic pulse. Kayla could already imagine how he would feel inside of her. Like a warm stream. Like a vibrator turned to its highest setting.

"I'm absolutely sure." Kayla sat back on the bed and pulled her legs up, keeping the panties stretched between her knees.

Swann stepped up and took a handful of her panties, holding onto them like reins on a horse. His other hand stroked his cock and directed it toward her hole.

"Put it in me!" Kayla breathed.

Swann obliged, pushing his hips so that his shaft was drenched in her wetness. He slid in so easily, with only her vaginal mucus as lube. She groaned, feeling a mounting orgasm stamp her chest. They hadn't even started fucking properly and she was already about to cum.

Standing at the foot of the bed, Swann scrunched his face up, tugged her panties, and began to hump her. His cock glided in and out in rhythmic turns. She felt a hot blast of pleasure scuttle across her pelvis.

Panic set upon Swann's face. He pulled out and immediately shot a dripping load of creamy syrup up her belly. His cum sped out of him like fire from the backside of a rocket. She gasped in joy at his ejaculation.

"I'm sorry!" He muttered. "I usually don't cum so fast—"

"It's the house. Look, you aren't even going soft yet! Put it back in!" Kayla declared.

Swann did as commanded, screwing his still seeping cock into her pussy. He fell upon her, thrusting in deep. He filled her cavern excitedly.

"Your right! I haven't even lost it!" Swann declared as he humped Kayla.

"Yes. Oh, God! You're so good, Swann!"

He reached down and squeezed her jiggling left breast. His grip was rough and stern. She liked the pain that shot through her as he started to pull at her flesh, working it as if it could rotate.

Then, he punched her. Hard. It wasn't playful, it was a mean crack to the nose. Kayla released a wet cough as she felt her face crumple inward.

"What the fuck!" Kayla sputtered, surprised and angered by the blow.

He clobbered her face again, causing her nose to give in and release two blasts of warm blood. Her fluids stippled her chest, like red sprinkles on a white cupcake.

"The *fuck,* Swann?" Kayla shouted. "Get the fuck off me!" She pushed against him, but he collapsed on top of her, driving the full length of his swollen cock into her. It hurt.

Kayla yipped with pain and tried to squirm away from him, but his hand latched around her throat and squeezed tightly. He was battering her face with punches.

His fist had turned into a blunt club, each blow filled Kayla's head with static.

This isn't right. Kayla thought. *We were just having fun. We were just fucking. Now... now...*

Swann put both hands around her throat and squeezed. She felt her esophagus turn hot and her belly ache. She realized that she was pissing herself. Urine drenched his still thrusting cock and squirted up his pelvis. She was embarrassed by her body's reaction, but there was nothing she could do to stop it. He fucked her regardless of her reddening face, her whitened eyes, and her simpering cries.

He released her when she was on the cusp of unconsciousness. Kayla came roaring back to reality, choking and coughing as if she had just swallowed smoke.

"Puh... puh—leeeeze." Kayla muttered.

He slapped her across the cheek. She turned her head against the bed and began to weep. All the while, he thrust in and out of her, relishing her tears.

"I'm sorry." Kayla eventually gasped, as if any of this was her fault.

"Shut up, cunt." Swann's voice was ice. He grabbed her hair and pulled. She felt him release a sticky wad of ejaculate inside her. It felt like acid. "I'm going to make you my cum dumpster." He seethed.

"N-no." Kayla moaned.

"'No' means 'yes' in this house." He chuckled as he hefted her up and carted her toward the X-frame. She faded in and out of consciousness as he secured her arms and legs to the medieval frame.

Swann stood back and admired his work.

Kayla's pussy was dripping with cum, urine, and blood. Her face was demolished. Her right eye was swollen shut and her lip had been lacerated. Blood fumed from her nostrils with each raspy breath. She could feel a welt growing on her crown.

Kayla looked toward her rapist. She loathed his snide smile and his stringy, sweat-besmirched hair. How had he gotten such a pleasant reputation in the industry, when in reality he was the worst kind of monster.

Swann's erection was still strong. He rubbed his horn and leered at her.

"Stop... this..." Kayla wheezed.

"I don't think I will." He said.

Kayla blinked—

—and suddenly, the room was no longer empty.

She could have screamed at the things she saw, but all of her energy was drained from her by the assault.

What had once been a sensual love-chamber had turned into what could only be described as a murderer's dungeon. There were chains hanging from the walls and ceiling, and dried out corpses dangled on skeletal arms from each manacle. Instead of a bed, there was now a putrid bath, filled with maggots and decapitated heads. All the body parts in the tub were stripped of flesh, and the maggots had churned up the bodies into a gunky paste, which smelled like raw sewage.

A man wearing a red robe was standing by a wooden platform, to which a young woman had been tied. She was incapable of screaming as her tongue and lower jaw had been removed and replaced with a red cave. Her pelvis was glimmering with needles. What must have been a thousand metallic pins had been pushed through her pubis, along the edges of her vagina, and into her anus. They looked like bushels of silver growing up from her groin.

The red-robed deviant was using a corkscrew to pulverize her right eye. Ocular pulp streamed out of her socket and gleamed along the ridges of her sallow cheek.

Kayla saw that the woman had had holes drilled into her brow as well, and she wondered if the woman was even capable of feeling pain anymore.

Another two women entered the chamber, laughing as they strolled arm-in-arm. They froze to observe the eye gouging before turning their attention to Kayla.

As they approached, Kayla saw that they were naked. Their nipples had been removed and they each had slashes grooved into their flattened bellies. They looked as if they had been hollowed out beneath their rib cages.

They shouldn't be alive, much less laughing.

Oh, but Kayla knew the truth. They weren't alive. They were ghosts.

All of us are, I think.

"This one's new!" One of the sneering ghosts said as she pointed to Kayla.

"Oh, I like her. She'll suffer nicely, won't she!"

They stood on either side of Swann, but he didn't seem to notice them. Instead, he held out a hand and grabbed Kayla's breast, squeezing it harshly. She tried to protest, but her words froze in her throat when a scream came from the maggot-bath. A bald man broke through the surface of the decayed porridge and puked up a payload of squirming maggots. He then sank back beneath the pool, vanishing from sight.

Kayla turned back to Swann and saw that he had been given a red-hot fire poker.

He nodded slowly.

"No!" Kayla wailed. "NO!"

Swann stooped down, adjusting the poker so that it was aimed directly between Kayla's trembling thighs.

"No!" Kayla screamed.

He penetrated her slowly. The searing poker seemed to slip into her vagina, melting the sensitive flesh inside and tearing into her tissues. She rocked her head back and let loose a primal scream.

The chamber of horrors matched her screams with multiple others.

But none were quite so loud as Swann's keening laughter.

CHAPTER NINE
GOD WANTS YOU TO HURT

Jace and Daisey sat in silence before realizing that Kayla, Geoff, and Swann had all gone missing. It was dark outside, and the moon was full. They heard rain pattering across the lawn.

"What do you think?" Daisey eventually asked. "Do we leave or—"

"I'm sure Geoff will be back any moment!" Jace rocked on her heels and looked toward the nearest window. "I'm sure of it!"

"Somethings wrong. It's obvious, isn't it? There's something bad going on and... and we oughta leave before it gets us." Daisey said.

'What do you mean?"

"I mean, this house is obviously haunted! You know it, but you aren't saying it out loud. C'mon, Jace. The weird hold it has on all of us can't be denied. But if we just leave then... then *it* can't get us."

Jace scratched her brow and sighed. "You're right. I know you're right. But... my brain is telling me to stay."

"I don't know if it's your brain saying that." Daisey said. "I don't want to sound crazy but—"

They heard someone thump down the stairs. Both women looked up and were surprised when Swann rounded the corner and walked casually into the parlor. He was naked, coated in blood, and he had stripped the flesh of Kayla's face from her skull. The detached face was planted to the center of his chest, glued by her coagulated blood.

At first, Jace thought that she was hallucinating. There was no way her leading man was actually standing before her, streaked in gore, and wearing her leading ladies face like a temporary tattoo on his chest. No way in hell!

Daisey screamed, planting her hands against the sides of her face.

Jace shouted: "Oh my god!"

Swann cocked his head, beamed, and said: "You need to come with me. You need to see... the suffering chamber!"

Jace raced around him. He didn't even move to catch her, simply letting Jace dash toward the door and away from his horrific appearance. Jace realized, as she swung the door open, that she had left Daisey in the parlor.

Concerns for her friend were forgotten when the door opened, and Geoff greeted her on the front lawn.

He was bloated, his body stuffed with wriggling fetuses which poked their limbs out from his tattered flesh. One had even managed to screw itself into his eye-socket, enlarging the side of his head to the point where any further pressure would cause it to burst.

Jace shrieked, retreating away from the horrendous sight of her camera man

Geoff took a lurching step forward. She saw two pairs of infant-feet sticking out of his mouth. His throat had ballooned like a bullfrog.

Geoff held up a decimated hand. It looked as if a dog had attacked it, biting away his fingers and tearing into his palm. Incapable of speech, Geoff released a zombified groan.

Jace turned away from him and caught sight of Swann. He was striding out of the parlor, dragging Daisey by the hair. She was bucking like a stallion, battering his sturdy hand with her fists.

"Let me go!" Daisey repeated, to no avail.

"You have to see it, Daisey!" Swann said as he began to haul her up the stairs. "It's *beautiful*!"

Jace turned back toward the door and saw that the yard was filled with mutilated figures. Naked women with slashed throats, battered faces, and skinned limbs stood like a distorted army. Jace couldn't even begin to count them all, but she was sure that their numbers reached the hundreds. The crowd surged forward as one, racing toward the Dobbsin house with malicious glee in their demented eyes. The wave of spirits began to swarm the doorway, and Jace had no choice but to race up the stairs and away from them.

She heard them crowd the lobby in a rush. Their footsteps were wet, and their laughter was wicked. Jace pushed past Swann and Daisey. As she went by, Swann swiped at her with a gore-soaked paw. He laughed as Jace flinched away from him, then shouted:

"God wants you to hurt, Jace! Why else would he have brought us here?"

"Help me, Jace! HELP ME!" Daisey screeched. "OH, GOD, JACE, FOR THE LOVE OF GOD, HELP ME!"

Jace ran up the stairs, crying as the tumultuous crowd of ghosts mocked her with their hysterical howling.

CHAPTER TEN
THE DEVIL'S WHORES

Jace felt as if she was locked in an unyielding nightmare.

How did any of this happen? None of it makes sense. The Magick Manor is killing us, oh God! It's killing us!

As she sprinted down the hall, she turned her head to look through the open doors of the rooms. Where there had once been empty, cold spaces, now there were torture chambers! Jace caught sight of red rooms, painted in gore and bloody sludge. She saw white faces, crisscrossed with gouging cuts and lacerations. As she went by each room, the activity halted as the ghosts looked up to watch her rush by.

"Stop!" Jace shouted, as if it was all a performance that could be paused. "Stop it, please!"

She reached the end of the hallway and vaulted up another flight of stairs, heading up to the third and final floor of Magick Manor. The air here felt hot and oppressive, so unlike the rest of the house.

Jace fell into Hell upon reaching the top of the stairs.

Holy shit. Jace thought as she skidded to an abrupt stop. The third floor was one expansive room, and it made the terrors she had previously witnessed look like a picnic.

The third floor was coated in gore. A thick paste lined the floor, ankle deep and churning with slithering snakes, worms, and centipedes. A literal orgy of creepy-crawlers.

There were meat hooks dangling from the ceiling and affixed to each one was a squirming body. Limbless, headless torsos drifted amid full-bodied sufferers. The carcasses ranged from the elderly to the unborn. Fetuses cried mournfully, black ink dripping from their toothless mouths.

Jace saw a woman hanging upside down by her ankles, her fingertips drifting above the fetid pool of writhing worms beneath her. Her belly was unzipped, and her pink intestines hung between her sagging breasts. Jace saw that her cheeks had been scraped away from her face, exposing two hollow holes that gave a naked view to her jutting teeth.

Her tongue poked out from the side of her face, a rosy, mangled rag of mid-masticated flesh.

"Jace!" Swann shouted from behind her.

She spun on her heels and looked down the stairs. Swann was striding up the steps, dragging Daisey behind him. Daisey was crying like a brokenhearted child, her hair being tugged roughly by her abuser.

"*Jaaaaaaace!*" Swann sang.

Jace held her breath, put her hands to her mouth, and stepped away from the stairs. Her feet sank into the pool of gore. Jace screamed and hopped around, as if she was being electrocuted. She saw a flatworm laying across he left foot, roiling against the flesh of her ankle.

Jace kicked and watched as the black creature flipped through the air before plopping into the ground.

Jace's back hit one of the dangling bodies. An arm looped instantly around her throat, securing her in place.

"No! Let me *go*!" Jace screeched and shoved against the body. She caught sight of an elderly man, his eyes gouged out, his teeth removed, and his throat held open by pins— like a dissected butterfly.

The old man chuckled, rotating on his meat-hook.

"Stop! Stop!" Jace held her hair in her hands and pulled. "Stop!"

The carcasses around her began to chitter with morbid laughter. *They weren't victims! They were willing participants in this endless horror show!*

"Stop!" Jace's throat broke with her cries. "Stop!"

She caught sight of several figures standing amidst the clusters of captive bodies. They slowly approached her, gliding across the viscous pool.

Jace froze, taking in their atrocious appearances. There were three of them, and they were almost recognizable. She had seen their images in the documentary about Magick Manor.

Salt Mortimer had her chest caved in. Her broken ribs stuck out like a row of white fence-posts along the center of her chest. Her blonde hair had been stained crimson.

Darren Armstrong was hobbling on broken legs. They had been snapped on their sockets and stretched out as if he was mid-way through a split stance. A knobby staff had been piked into his bleeding anus and bulged from his toothless mouth. He looked like spit-roasted meat.

Frank Mortimer had nails pounded through the top of his head. The rusty protrusions had been twisted, churning his gray brains up and forcing them out from his ears and his empty eye sockets. He sneezed, and Jace saw a cloud of pink mist jet out from his nostrils.

"No!" Jace said, her voice cracked with horror. "No!"

"We are the Whores of Satan." Salt said in a toneless drawl. "The Lords and Mistresses of Hell. Come to us, Jace. Embrace the pleasures of eternity. Of mortification!"

Jace screamed. Tears seeped down her cheeks and into her opened mouth. She stepped backward, away from the encroaching terrors.

"Join us!" Frank growled, raising his hands and revealing skinless fingers. The whitened bones stuck out like gleaming claws. "Join the orgy!"

Jace closed her eyes. *I wanna go home. I wanna go home. I wanna go home—*

Swann grabbed her by the nape of her neck. His squeezing clutch sent bolts of panic down her spine. Jace squirmed helplessly as he dragged her into his chest.

"You'll do as you're told!" Swann snarled.

"Jace! Run!" Daisey said from Swann's other hand.

"Shut up!" Swann jerked her hair. "You shut up and do as you are *told*!"

Jace reached back and dug her fingers into Swann's face. Her nails punctured his eye. She felt a hot squirt of ocular secretions fill her palm.

Swann released her and Daisey. He reached up and clawed at his wounded face, crying out in a high-pitched tone that Jace wouldn't have thought him capable of. Like a roaring teakettle, his screech pitched higher and higher as his hands were gloved in his flowing blood.

"You... *bitch!*" Swann squealed.

Daisey shouldered him and he tumbled backward. Swann landed on his rump in the gore-stew beneath him. He began to scramble around like an overturned crab, slipping and sliding in the mucus and membrane topped puddle.

Daisey grabbed Jace's hand and yanked her toward the stairs. "c'mon! We need to go!"

Jace didn't need to be told twice.

Both girls froze midway down the stairs when they caught sight of what was waiting at the bottom. A creature that looked like a man was standing on all fours. Its arms were knobbed with scabs—like overfed ticks. Its bald head was red with pimples, each one filled with solidified curds. Its face was blank. It had neither mouth nor eyes. Instead, all there was at its center was a singular nostril, caked with dried and crusted snot.

Hanging from its pelvis were two penises. The organs were tipped with blackened barbs.

"Holy shit!" Daisey sneered.

The creature began to lope up the stairs, snuffling out its loathsome, rotted nose.

Jace and Daisey turned and saw Swann standing at the top of the stairs. Kayla's face was still pinned to his chest, and his right eye was flattened. His left eye had turned red with rage. His teeth were clenched, and his lips were raised so that they could see his gums.

"I'll kill you, you *bitch*!" Swann promised.

Jace heard a whoosh of hot air as the beast landed behind her. She whirled around, but not before the creature latched onto Daisey.

"No!" Daisey screamed as the thing dragged her down the steps. "No! Let me go! Oh, GOD!"

Jace was then struck in the head by Swann. She fell unconscious before she slammed against the steps and rolled down to their bottom.

∗∗MAGICK∗∗

CHAPTER ELEVEN
BROTHEL

When Jace opened her eyes, she was strapped to a wicker chair. She was still on the third floor, and the horrors had intensified. The zombified corpses had all moved up here, and they were fucking in wet clumps. She scanned the room, watching as fists glided into puckered rectums. Mouths were cracked open so more organs could be fit into them. She could see a man without hands being anally penetrated by a creature that looked like a human-warthog hybrid. Its tusks drooled snot, which it took in its hand and used to grease its two-foot long erection.

A body was torn from its meat-hook, and the wound where the hook had penetrated it was then used as a faux-cunt. Maggots were being crammed into any available orifice. Gore was draining from freshly carved holes.

A creature that looked like a fat woman with multiple sets of eyes was pulling the bones out of a body. She snapped each bone with a snickering *crack*. She upturned the fractured chutes and drained their marrow out onto her sluggish tongue.

She watched as a woman was asphyxiated with her own organs while another woman blasted her face with blood-tinted urine.

Jace watched as a limbless woman with a metallic funnel stuffed down her maw greedily accepted an offering of greasy fecal matter from the asshole of a headless torso.

Jace felt as if she was going mad. The orgy of depravity persisted despite its impossibilities. Swann took her shoulders and rubbed. He had been standing behind her, waiting for her to be roused from her slumber.

"It's gorgeous, isn't it?" He said cheerfully.

"Oh, God!' Jace moaned as she watched a pregnant woman squat. Her fetus came tumbling too quickly from her vault. It was gray and mushy, having died in her womb and fermented in its embryonic prison. Upon flopping against the ground, a dwarf fell upon it and began to chew the soft meat of the fetus's armpit. The dwarf ate greedily, yipping as the flesh tore away from the miscarriage.

"I-it's terrible!" Jace said. "It's horrible!"

"It's Hell." Swann confirmed. "You know what this is, Jace? You know what this really is?"

Swann stepped in front of her, holding onto her lashed arms and grinning into Jace's tear-stained eyes.

"It's a brothel!" He nodded vigorously. "Dobbsin... he built this house to be a brothel... and it's been one ever since!"

"What do you mean?!" Jace wept.

"This is where demons come to FUCK!" Swann chirped with mirth. "This is where they come... to fuck the living and the dead!"

Daisey screamed. Her recognizable voice rose from the swamp of bodies and sent shudders of revulsion through Jace. Jace scanned the orgy, seeking her friend.

Daisey was kneeling in the center of the room. One half of her face had melted. The flesh hung in gunky dollops from the bone, streaming down in white strands. The other half of her face had been burned to a crackling crisp.

Her arms had been removed, leaving hollow holes beside her shoulders. Bits of red gristle hung from the wounds, each one a clump of gore interlaced with black tissue. Her left breast had been skinned. Yellow fat curdled beneath the purpled musculature.

Daisey was being masturbated on by a circle of demons. Each one looked more loathsome than the last; some were female, and others were male, and others were so malformed it was hard to tell.

A fat demon with an anus for a mouth and a scrotum that looked like a bushel or ripe grapes ejaculated on Daisey's back. Steam sizzled from her flesh, burning under the weight of the demon's vile cum!

Jace sobbed. She tilted her head toward her chest and began to tremor spasmodically, as if she was on an electric chair.

"It's the most beautiful thing I've ever seen." Swann said.

"No! No! No!" Jace wailed. "I just wanna go h-h-home!"

"And you will!" Swann grabbed her cheeks and lifted her head, so she was looking directly into his crazed eyeball. She saw a fuzzy caterpillar crawling out from the socket she had torn apart with her fingers. "You'll go home, Jace. You won't be kept here. Hell has a favor to ask of you."

"W-what?" Jace asked.

"We want you to do your job, Jace." Swann said. Another caterpillar was making its way out of his mouth. It inched down his chin before falling into Jace's lap. "We want you... to *film* this!"

"Jace, *help!*" Daisey screamed as another dollop of acidic cum landed on her dome. Her flesh receded from the spot where the demon had laid his putrid seed.

"What?" Jace couldn't believe what she was hearing. "What do you mean?"

Swann only grinned in response. He hooked his fingers under her restraints and pulled them loose, freeing Jace from her wicker chair. She remained frozen in place, mortified by her surroundings and by the offensive offer.

"I don't—I don't know what you want me to do!"

Swann grabbed her hand by the wrist and jerked it up. A demon with an elephantine trunk plodded over, carrying Geoff's camera in its scaly fingers. He delicately set the camera into Jace's hand before slinking away.

Swann held Jace's face and said: "All we want... is a film. We just want something we can treasure... something we can watch in Hell until the end of days."

"This is... this is evil!"

"Yes!" Swann declared, standing up and spreading his arms wide. "And its your job to film it! You're a trailblazer Jace! You aren't just filming the first porno in a haunted house... you're filming it in Hell itself!"

Swann pitched forward and unleashed a vomitous stream. Yellowed bile, wriggling caterpillars, and gunky bits or organic matter fell out of his mouth in a vicious gush.

Jace threw the camera. It landed in the midst of his pool.

"I won't do it! I'd rather die than film this!" Jace attested. "I'd rather die—"

"You'll die forever then!" Swann swiped at her with one hand while the other cupped his mouth. More vomit spilled out between his fingers, a literal flood of puke!

"NO!" Jace threw a punch. It collided with Swann's hand and stamped it into his mouth. He stumbled backward, surprised by the blow.

Jace struck while the iron was hot. She rushed Swann, battering his face with slaps and punches. He stumbled on the wet floor, crashing backward.

Jace pounced upon him, taking his head in her hands and slammed it repeatedly against the floor. More vomit exploded from his mouth, spattering Jace's chest and filling her own oral cavity. Jace clenched her teeth and continued to pound into Swann's head.

"You... can't... make... me!" Jace screeched.

"This is Hell!" Swann said. "I can do... whatever the *fuck*... I want!"

All around them, the demons exclaimed in rapturous joy. They were loving the fight between the demented mortals. It even made them redirect their attention away from the half-melted and collapsed Daisey—whose mouth was so deformed she could do nothing more than gurgle.

Jace dug her fingers into Swann's remaining eye. This time, he only laughed as his orb collapsed and was pulped by Jace's molesting digits.

Jace stood and began to drag Swann across the bloody ground, tugging at the top portion of his skull by hooking her fingers into both of his empty sockets. Swann continued to laugh, even as he kicked and squirmed.

"This... stops... now!" Jace said.

Swann began to choke with laughter, even as Jace hauled him up to a sitting position, hooked her arms around him, and lifted him up to his feet. Jace heaved and dropped Swann directly into a limp meat hook. The metal implement punctured the back of Swann's head and jutted out of his mouth, knocking his front teeth loose. The white buds fell onto the ground like a handful of pebbles.

Speared through the back of the head by a rusty hook, Swann should have died, but he rotated in place, his neck stretched by the weight of his body and his arms flailing by his sides. He was still laughing!

Jace roared in anger, grabbed Swann's arms, and yanked downward. The force of her weight combined with his own drove the protrusion up. The hook split Swann's head neatly in half, releasing a guttural blast of blood and brain matter as the top of Swann's skull was divided.

"Fuck you!" Jace screeched. "Fuck you! Fuck you!"

She began to dance on his body, stomping her feet into his fractured skull and mulching it into a bone-speckled paste. Blood sputtered out from his yawning gullet. His arms and fingers twitched, and his bowels were voided. Sheets of fecal fluids sprayed out between his vibrating thighs.

"Fuck you! Fuck you! Fuck you!" Jace began to howl like a maddened animal. She was driven into a frenzied glee by the cathartic bloodshed. The demons all watched in stupefied bewilderment as Jace hunkered down and began to grab handfuls of Swann's annihilated skull. She began to slam the twisted strands of brain matter into her mouth, chewing happily.

Around a mouthful of pulped brain parts, Jace turned and screamed:

"Fuck... you!"

The demons and ghosts all cheered. Their applause sounded like an encroaching storm. Their calloused, blood smeared hands smacked wetly as they hooted, cried out, and jeered.

Jace turned her head and snarled. Her teeth were stained with Swann's brain. Gore dribbled down her chin and filled the bowl of her clavicle.

Jace stood, tightening her fists at her sides. She shook her head, as if she could reject her atrocious surroundings. The applause tapered off, and before long the only present noise came from the churning maggots, writhing worms, and plinking blood.

"I... I just wanna go home." Jace said.

A voice crept into her hear. It sounded like gravel.

"You are home."

CHAPTER TWELVE

THE DOBBSIN HOUSE

FOREVER AFTER

Magick Manor was closed. The doors and windows were all sealed, and no one dared approach it. Not since a group of pornographers had gone to it, only to disappear that very night. There were no answers, but there were speculative guesses. The house was haunted, and it had consumed all who entered it. It was, frankly, foolhardy for one to even presume they would be allowed exit simply because they had been allowed entrance.

Magick Manor was closed, but only because it was sleeping. Satiated by its meal, it would wait patiently before it was ready to welcome new guests.

Inside, Jace couldn't wait to film what became of those unlucky bastards that followed her lead. She remembered little of her own life. Being a ghost was like living in a constant state of adrenaline fueled rage. All she saw was Swann's destruction, her own terror, and the bewildering images the demons had shown her on the third floor.

Holding the camera, at the very least, gave her some sense of purpose. However slight, she knew that if she recorded whatever she saw, then maybe it would eventually become manageable to her fragmented psyche.

This house is haunted. It's haunted... by me. Jace thought as she drifted from room to room, her camera held to her eye...

...capturing Hell in all its glory.

✲✲THE END✲✲

⁎⁎MAGICK⁎⁎

∴MAGICK∴

⁂MAGICK⁂

AFTERWORD

I love challenging myself, which is why I wrote *No One Rides For Free* with a caveat. That book had to be written, edited, and published in ten days. The reception it received was warm, and I enjoyed the frenzied nature of the project so much... I just couldn't wait to do it again. And so, I bought a random cover from Christy Aldridge and decided to do the ten day challenge again. And thus, *MAGICK* was born.

Like a lot of my books, this was influenced by my love for Italian cinema. Italian horror movies tend to work on the principle that "if it looks good, it's going in the movie". There doesn't have to be logic, or even a plot. Just some crazy shit happening at random, with loads of atmosphere and creativity on display.

✱✱MAGICK✱✱

So, which Italian movies inspired *Magick*?

I think you'll find bits and pieces of *Ghost House, House by the Cemetery, Beyond Darkness,* and *Witchery* on full display here! And yes, I recommend each and every one of those bizarre, weirdo, and gore-soaked flicks!

And I exclusively listened to scores by the great Carla Maria Cordio as I wrote. Lemme tell you, those Italian film scores are so conducive to this style of writing. I really let the music design the scenes as I went! I strongly suggest you always listen to Italian scores while reading my books. Fabio Frizzi and Goblin are both great places to start if you need a suggestion!

Magick was written in conjunction with another book, and I do think the two will make an excellent double feature. Jessie Seitz saw my announcement that I was doing a ten day project, felt inspired, and asked to join me on this journey! Her book is called *SANDRA*, and it's a supernatural revenge yarn. If you haven't heard of Jessie Seitz, she did the incredible special effects for the vampire-splatter flick *Jakob's Wife*... which you can and should watch on Shudder if you haven't already. She's also directing the sixth installment of Stephen Biro's American Guinea Pig series. The title for her film is called Chum-Bucket so... you know you're in extreme hands with whatever she writes.

So, be sure and read *SANDRA* as soon as you can!

And thank you so, so much, Jessie, for joining me on this nasty adventure!

A few more folks to thank:

Thank you to Makency Hudson for your tireless work on this book. I'm so thankful you're willing to edit something under such a maddening deadline! Also, you're just the best human on the planet so... Thank you!

Thank you to Christy Aldridge! Not only are you an amazing artist but are *so* caring and encouraging too! You always cheer me up and I'm thankful to know you!

Thank you to everyone on Facebook, Twitter, and Instagram for hyping up this project and all my other endeavors! Jack Burner, Don Taylor, Corrina Morse, Angel Van Atta, Eamon Dingle, Travis Davis, Russell Holbrook, Donna Owens, Margaret Hamnett, and so... so... so many more! You all make me feel so honored and humbled by your praise and kindness!

Thank you to Melissa, so convincing me that vomiting caterpillars would be way nastier than spiders.

Thank you to you, my dear reader! Your support means the world to me!

With Love,
JUDITH SONNET

Do you like extreme horror? Splatterpunk? Bizzaro? Indie books and authors?

If yes, then the best thing you can do for us is leave a review on whatever platform you can! Goodreads! Amazon! TikTok! Facebook! Instagram!

We survive on word-of-mouth. the more talked about we are, the more chances we have to write this disgusting shit without fear of censorship!

Help an author... LEAVE A REVIEW AND WE'LL LOVE YOU FOREVER!

⁘MAGICK⁘

For editing inquiries, contact Makency Hudson at her website:

Bookmenace.com
You can also reach her via email:
Makency@bookmenace.com

Makency Hudson is an amazing editor and a hard worker. I couldn't have done this without her help, patience, and determination.

Printed in Great Britain
by Amazon